FROGGY'S SLEEPOVER

FROGGY'S SLEEPOVER

by JONATHAN LONDON
illustrated by FRANK REMKIEWICZ

SCHOLASTIC INC.

New York Toronto London Auckland Sydney
Mexico City New Delhi Hong Kong Buenos Aires

For Max and Sean, longtime overnighters.
  —J. L.

For Austin and Anthony, my sleepover pals.
  —F. R.

ISBN 0-439-80093-5

Text copyright © 2005 by Jonathan London. Illustrations copyright © 2005 by Frank Remkiewicz.
All rights reserved. Published by Scholastic Inc., 557 Broadway, New York, NY 10012, by arrangement with
Viking Children's Books, a member of Penguin Group (USA) Inc. SCHOLASTIC and associated
logos are trademarks and/or registered trademarks of Scholastic Inc.

12 11 10 9 8 7 6 5 4 3 2 1   5 6 7 8 9 10/0

Printed in the U.S.A.   40

First Scholastic printing, September 2005

Set in Kabel

It was Friday,
and school was out.
Froggy flopped home
from the school bus—
flop flop flop—
singing, "Hurray! Hurray!
It's Friday! Friday! I'm going to
Max's for a sleepover!"

"That's great!" said Froggy's mother. And she gave him a plate of chocolate fly cookies. "This is your first sleepover! Are you nervous?"

"Who, me? Of course not!" said Froggy.
And he hopped up and flopped to his room—
flop flop flop.

He pulled
a big sack from
his closet—*slam!*

Stuffed in his
sleeping bag—*sloof!*

Squeezed in
his pillow—
poof!

Slapped in his
pajamas—*puff!*

Shoved in a pair
of underwear—
pum!

"Oops!" said Froggy,
and flopped back inside—*flop flop flop!*
"I found it!" he yelled.
"It was in the cookie jar!"—
slam!

Then out the door he went,
dragging his sack behind him—*shlooop!*

FRROOGGYY!

called his mother.
"Wha-a-a-t?"
"Did you forget your toothbrush?"
"Oops!" said Froggy,
and flopped back inside—*flop flop flop.*
"I found it!" yelled Froggy.
"It was in my toy chest!"—
bang!

"Don't forget to brush!" said his mother.
"I know!" said Froggy.

Then off he went to Max's,
dragging his sack behind him—*shlooop!*

At Max's, he dumped everything out on the floor—*shlump!*

Rolled out his sleeping bag—*sloof!*

And fluffed out his pillow—*floof!*

"Okay," said Froggy. "I'm ready for bed!"

"But Froggy," said Max, "it's only four o'clock!"

So they waited till after dinner, then
they crawled into their sleeping bags.
"Wait!" said Froggy, jumping up.
"I forgot to brush my teeth!"

"Don't be a baby!" said Max.
"This is a sleepover.
You don't have to brush!"

Froggy crawled back into his bag.
"Wait!" he said, jumping back up.
"I need my huggy to go to sleep!"
"Sleep?" said Max. "Who's going to sleep?
We can tell scary stories
and have pillow fights all night long!"

Froggy slipped back into his bag,
and Max told a story that made Froggy's skin crawl.

"Now it's your turn," said Max.
But there were weird scr-e-e-e-ching sounds.
And scary shapes hung in the shadows like ghosts.

"I have a better idea!" said Froggy.
"What?" said Max.
"Let's go to *my* house
for a sleepover!"

When they got back to Froggy's,
they tiptoed inside in the dark.
Quiet . . . quiet . . .

CRASH !

Froggy bumped into a lamp
and knocked over the
goldfish bowl—*splash!*

FRROOGGYY!

yelled his mother. "What's all the ruckus?" She flicked on the light.

"Oops!" cried Froggy, looking more red in the face than green. "We decided to sleep here, instead."

"Oh, Froggy," said his mother.
"I thought you wanted to sleep at Max's."
"I *did*!" cried Froggy.
"But . . . um . . . I was hungry!
And you make the best popcorn!

"Can you make us some? Ple-e-e-a-se?"
"Okay, you little munchkins,"
said his mom.

Pop pop pop!
She made them some
buttery popcorn,
then went back
to bed.

Plump plump plump!
Froggy and Max were having
a wild pillow fight.

"GOOD NIGHT, PUDDINGHEADS!" called Froggy's mom.
"I hope they go to sleep soon," groaned Froggy's dad.
"Me, too," moaned Froggy's mom.

Froggy's parents were snoring like horses
when Froggy's mom heard a sound.
Her eyes popped open,
and she flicked on the light.
Max was standing by the bed.
"I have a tummy ache," he said.
"I want to go home!"

So back they went to Max's,
dragging their sacks behind them—*shloop!*

But there were still weird sounds and scary shadows there . . .
so they went back to Froggy's.

But Max wanted his own pillow . . .
so they went back to Max's.

But Froggy wanted pink lemonade . . .
so back and forth they went—
shlooop shlooop shlooop! . . .

till at last they fell asleep at Max's house—
at nine o'clock in the morning.
Zzzzzzzzzzzzz . . .